HATCHIMALS™
ADVENTURE TO
WISHING STAR WATERFALL

by Leigh Olsen
illustrated by Kellee Riley

PENGUIN YOUNG READERS LICENSES
An Imprint of Penguin Random House LLC

ISBN 9781524783839   10 9 8 7 6 5 4 3 2 1

The magnolia tree had been in Ava and Oliver's backyard for as long as they could remember. But earlier that summer, there'd been something unusual about it. Ava found a gleaming white egg dotted with pink and teal speckles in a hollow at the tree's roots. Her younger brother, Oliver, found one with purple speckles.

They could tell the eggs held living creatures—they could hear heartbeats coming from inside! When Ava and Oliver tapped the eggs, the creatures tapped back. It was a marvelous mystery! Eventually, with lots of love and hugs from the kids, the creatures hatched! One was a pink-furred Penguala with webbed feet and the other was a blue-beaked purple Draggle with scales down his back! Ava named the Penguala Pippi, and Oliver called the Draggle Duke.

Ava and Oliver had taken care of their new friends ever since. And today an adventure was in store. Pippi tugged on Ava's capris, pointing to the tree. "What is it?" Ava asked. Pippi took off, cooing with excitement as Ava followed. "Wait for me!" Ava shouted with a laugh.

Oliver ran over with Duke. *Tat-a-tat!* Duke tapped on Oliver's leg. *Tat-a-tat!*

"Sorry, Duke," said Oliver. "I don't understand!"

"I've got it!" Ava exclaimed. "Remember how Pippi and Duke tapped from inside their eggs? Now they want us to tap the tree!"

Together they reached out and tapped the trunk three times: *Tap! Tap! Tap!*

Suddenly, the glowing outline of a tiny doorway appeared in the tree. Ava gave the door a gentle push, and all the colors of the rainbow poured out, revealing a dreamlike world on the other side.

"Whoa. That's amazing!" Oliver gasped. Ava stuck her hand through the doorway, and as she did, her hand got smaller and fit easily! Pippi grabbed Ava's other hand, and together they leaped through.

"Hooray, we're here!" Pippi shouted.

"Oh, Pippi!" Ava cried out in surprise. "You can talk!" She was also delighted to see that Pippi was bigger—she now reached Ava's waist!

Oliver and Duke tumbled in after them. "Wow," Oliver murmured in awe. "This is the most wonderful place I've ever seen! Those flowers look like giant lollipops. I almost want to take a bite!" The kids darted from glittery oversized blossoms to bright buttercups that dripped with real butter. In the distance, a crashing waterfall glimmered. They could feel the magic in the air!

"Hello!" exclaimed a sweet voice. Ava and Oliver turned to see a furry creature. She had silvery wings and the friendly face of a koala. "Welcome to Hatchtopia, home of the Hatchimals!"

"Hatchimals?" asked Ava. "Are *you* a Hatchimal?"

"Yes, and so are they," the creature said, pointing to Pippi and Duke. "My name's Kiki—I'm a Koalabee. That great big tree is the Giggling Tree." They'd entered through the magnolia, but the other side of the door was in a much larger, more dazzling tree. It was clearly a magical door from their world to this extraordinary place!

"The Giggling Tree is quite important to us," Kiki explained. "It helps spread laughter and cheer throughout Hatchtopia."

"I *do* feel very happy," said Oliver.

"Me too!" said Ava.

"I'm gathering three newborn Hatchimals and taking them to Wishing Star Waterfall," said Kiki. "Would you like to help?"

"We'd love to!" said Ava. "But why Wishing Star Waterfall?"

"It's an astonishing place that catches shooting stars in its waters," said Kiki. She explained that all new Hatchimals got to slide down the waterfall and make their very first wish.

"Wow," Oliver whispered.

"And to thank you for helping, you four can each make a wish, too!" said Kiki.

"Ollie, what should we wish for?" Ava asked.

"I don't know!" he said. "But we'd better start thinking!"

Kiki the Koalabee led them to a lake of purple water. The water shifted from a lavender shade to a deep plum. "This is Lilac Lake!" she said. Kiki walked over to a nest of pink flowers and gazed inside. "It looks like our newest friend has just hatched!" she announced. "Love brings each Hatchimal to life. When the heart in the middle of the egg changes from purple to pink, that's when you know it's ready to hatch!"

Oliver peered inside the nest. A baby Hatchimal was making her way out of the shell.

"A Lilac Bunwee!" said Kiki. "We'll call you Bella." Bella the Bunwee cooed sweetly, making Ava laugh.

Oliver dipped his hand into the lake's water, turning it purple. "Maybe I'll wish for a pool filled with magical purple water!" he said.

After a hike into the mountains, they came upon spectacular glassy cliffs that dropped off into a deep valley below. "Welcome to Crystal Canyon," Kiki said, "the most enchanted place in Hatchtopia."

"I've never seen anything like it," said Ava, awestruck.

Nearby, a Hatchimal with the face of a cheetah hopped around. "A Cheetree! How cute," Kiki gushed. "Why don't we call him Charlie?"

"Charlie, will you please come with us to Wishing Star Waterfall?" Charlie the Cheetree nodded shyly.

"Maybe I'll wish for a necklace made from Crystal Canyon gems so I never forget this place!" said Ava.

"Next stop is Cloud Cove," said Kiki. "That's where we'll find the last new Hatchimal. And I need *your* help to get Ava and Oliver there!"

The Hatchimals grabbed hold of the kids' arms and flapped their wings, lifting Ava and Oliver up into the sky!

After a breathtaking journey, the Hatchimals set Ava and Oliver down on a stretch of soft clouds.

"This is Cloud Cove," said Kiki. "We're near the top of Wishing Star Waterfall, where all the best flyers in Hatchtopia hang out. The more the Hatchimals fly here, the softer they become!"
Ava and Oliver bounced from one fluffy white puff to another, searching for the final addition to their group.

"Oh no," said Ava. "I don't see anyone!"

"Where can that last Hatchimal be?" asked Oliver.

Everyone searched the wispy clouds, but the Hatchimal was nowhere in sight! All hope seemed lost. Just then, Oliver and Duke rushed over to the group.

"Come quick!" Oliver urged. "We couldn't find the Hatchimal because it hasn't hatched yet! It's still inside its egg, hidden in a puffy cloud, and it needs our help."

Oliver led everyone to the egg. They all leaned in close, rubbing and hugging it. Oliver patted the shell gently.

Tap-tap. Tap-tap-tap.

"It's hatching!" Oliver shouted.

A pony-like creature emerged from the egg. "A Ponette!" Kiki exclaimed. "We'll call you Poppy."

"Hatchy Birthday, Poppy!" everyone shouted.

At last, it was time to slide down Wishing Star Waterfall and make their wishes.

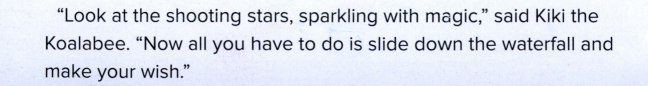

"Look at the shooting stars, sparkling with magic," said Kiki the Koalabee. "Now all you have to do is slide down the waterfall and make your wish."

Bella, Charlie, and Poppy slid down gleefully. Pippi and Duke nodded at the kids to go next.

"On the count of three," said Ava, grabbing Oliver's hand. "One, two . . ."

". . . three!"

Ava and Oliver leaped, and the water whooshed them downward.

"I wish for a map of Hatchtopia," Ava shouted, "so I can come back and explore!"

"I wish for time to stand still in our world while we're here," exclaimed Oliver. "That way we can stay and play even longer next time!"

Ava and Oliver plunged into the lake at the bottom of the falls. Pippi and Duke followed, giggling. "I wish for the power to go to Hatchtopia whenever we want!" said Duke.

"And I wish for us all to be Hatch Friends Forever!" Pippi proclaimed.

"We'd better go home," Ava said while they dried off. "Mom and Dad will be wondering where we are."

"Thank you for showing us around your world," Oliver said to Kiki the Koalabee.

"We can't wait to come back soon!" Ava added.

"There are always more adventures to be had in Hatchtopia," said Kiki. "Hatch ya later!"